To Isobel and Alasdair
J.A.

First North American edition published in 2012 by Boxer Books Limited.

First published in Great Britain in 2012
by Boxer Books Limited.
www.boxerbooks.com

Text and illustrations copyright © 2012 Jonathan Allen

The illustrations were prepared digitally by the author
The text is set in Adobe Garamond Regular

ISBN 978-1-907967-30-6

1 3 5 7 9 10 8 6 4 2

Printed in China

All of our papers are sourced from managed forests and renewable resources.

# I'm not Sleepy!

## Jonathan Allen

Boxer Books

Baby Owl had stayed up all night, as every owl does.

And he looked very sleepy.

"Bedtime for a sleepy Baby Owl!"
called Mom.

"I'm not sleepy!" grumbled Baby Owl.

But he couldn't help giving
a great BIG s t r e t c h .
Then along bounced
Grey Squirrel.

"Well, you look sleepy to me,
Baby Owl!" said Grey Squirrel.

"I'm not sleepy!" said Baby Owl.

"I was just stretching my wings," said Baby Owl. "I will be learning to fly soon, you know."

Baby Owl settled back on his perch
and yawned a great BIG yawn.

"That was a VERY big yawn!"
said Mouse. "What a sleepy
Baby Owl you are this morning."

"I'm not sleepy!" said Baby Owl.
"I was just yawning because I am bored.
Owls need lots of excitement, you know."

Baby Owl settled back on his perch. And before long, his head started to nod and his eyelids began to droop.

Then along came Woodpecker.

"WAAA!"
said Baby Owl.

"Oops, sorry!" said Woodpecker, "I didn't know there was a sleepy Baby Owl on the other side of this tree."

"I am NOT sleepy!" shouted Baby Owl. "I was thinking. Owls are very wise, and we spend lots of time thinking, you know."

Then along came Dad.
"You look VERY sleepy, Baby Owl,"
said Dad. "It's time you were in bed."

"But I'm not sleepy!" cried Baby Owl.
"Everyone keeps telling me that I am,
but I'm not! I'm thinking!"

"I'm thinking too, Baby Owl,"
said Dad, lifting Baby Owl
from his branch.

"And I'm thinking that, sleepy or not,
you are certainly very grumpy.
Come in now, and I will read
you a bedtime story."